SCARLETT ANGELINA WOLVERTON-MANNING

JACQUELINE K. OGBURN   *pictures by* BRIAN AJHAR

DIAL BOOKS FOR YOUNG READERS *New York*

To my parents, Jack and Peggy Ogburn,
who told me I was smart as well as very beautiful
J. K. O.

To Mom for all the encouragement
and to Dad for all the strength
B. A.

Scarlett Angelina Wolverton-Manning lived in a very big house with her parents, the cook, the upstairs maid, the downstairs maid, the chauffeur, and the gardener. The house had a long driveway, a large lawn, and forty-seven rooms.

Her parents loved Scarlett Angelina very much and thought she was very beautiful. "She has the Wolverton smile," said her mama.

"She has the Manning eyes," said her papa.

And it was true.
In the long front par-
lor hung portraits
of the Wolvertons,
and they all had
big toothy smiles,
just like Scarlett
Angelina.

In the grand ball-
room hung portraits
of the Mannings,
and they all had big
fine eyes, just like
Scarlett Angelina.

Scarlett Angelina had no brothers or sisters, but she was too busy to be lonely. She took violin lessons, ballet lessons, swimming lessons, and on Tuesdays and Thursdays she had French lessons with a private tutor in the front parlor.

She rode to and from school and her lessons in a long black car.

One afternoon as she was looking out the window of the long black car, Scarlett Angelina noticed that they had driven past her house.

"Falstaff," she said, "you drove past my house. I will be late for my French lesson."

"My name is Ralph, and you're not going to any lesson today," the driver told her.

"Good," said Scarlett Angelina. "I didn't do my homework on pluperfect verbs anyway. Where are we going?"

"You're going to stay with me for a while, kid. Just do what I say and everything will be fine. Understand?" Ralph said.

"Just as long as you take me home soon. My mother says I always have to be home before dark," Scarlett Angelina replied, bouncing up and down on the backseat.

They drove out into the country, through the woods, and stopped next to a very small house.

Scarlett Angelina waited patiently in the backseat until Ralph opened the door for her and then they went inside.

The house had five rooms and no maids. The living room had a couch, two chairs, a green parrot, a goldfish, and a ginger cat. Scarlett Angelina said, "Nice kitty!" but the cat hissed and ran away.

"I'm hungry," announced Scarlett Angelina. "I always have steak, extra rare, for dinner on Thursdays. I will stay and dine with you— but you must take me home before dark."

"I think I have some hamburger in the fridge. You stay here and be quiet," Ralph told her. And he left Scarlett Angelina in the living room.

Scarlett Angelina smiled the famous Wolverton smile and said, "What a pretty birdie." The bird let out a horrible squawk and the cat hid behind a chair.

In the kitchen, Ralph was calling Scarlett Angelina's parents. The Wolverton-Manning household had been upset ever since Scarlett Angelina had not come home in time for her French lesson. The maids could not clean, the cook could not cook, and the gardener watered the cactus by mistake. Her parents were waiting anxiously by the telephone when it rang.

"Listen," Ralph whispered. "I have your kid, and I want five million dollars to bring her back."

"Oh dear, we have been so worried! Is she all right?" cried Mr. Wolverton-Manning. "Of course we want her back immediately, and I do believe we have that much money in the upstairs safe. But we must have her back before dark."

"That's what she keeps saying, but she may have to stay up past her bedtime tonight. You have to do what I say—and don't call the police," ordered Ralph.

"Of course, no police. But you don't understand, we must have her home before dark. She—she—she has to take her medicine before then—that's it, her medicine," stammered the distraught Mr. Wolverton-Manning.

"Okay, at seven-thirty then, that's sunset. Meet me at the Sweet Rest Graveyard by the tomb of Feris Wolfschmidt. You'd better be there with the money! And remember, no police," Ralph insisted.

"Oh, no, no police, never the police. We'll both be there." Mr. Wolverton-Manning hung up the phone and turned to his wife. "This is terrible! Our poor Scarlett Angelina! And tonight of all nights, when there is a full moon!"

"We must be brave, my darling," said Mrs. Wolverton-Manning. "We will get her back safely."

When Ralph went back to the living room, he found the bird cage on the floor.

"The birdie wanted out, so I opened the cage," said Scarlett Angelina, hiding a feather behind her back. "Where is my dinner?"

"It's still cooking," said Ralph.

Then he frowned. "You shouldn't have let Polly out, kid. I'll have trouble catching her and putting her back. I'll go get the burgers now. Do you like ketchup?"

"No ketchup, thank you, it will be red enough," she told him.

"What a lovely goldfish," Scarlett said sweetly as Ralph left the room.

Ralph came back with their dinner. "How did all this water get on the floor?"

"Oh, the cat knocked over the goldfish bowl," explained Scarlett Angelina, stuffing a piece of seaweed into her pocket. "She must have eaten the poor fishy."

"Fluffy never did that before. Bad Fluffy!" Ralph said, shaking his finger at the cat. "Eat your dinner, kid." Scarlett Angelina ate her hamburger in three big bites and carefully wiped her mouth with her napkin.

"Could I have some warm milk?" asked Scarlett Angelina. As Ralph went back to the kitchen, she got down to look behind the couch. "Here kitty, kitty."

"What happened to my couch?" cried Ralph.

"Oh, I was petting Fluffy, but she scratched me and ran away. She must be hiding now," said Scarlett Angelina, covering up a small ginger-colored patch of fur with her shoe.

"Drink your milk. And hurry up, we have to go," ordered Ralph.

They got back into the long black car and Ralph drove to the Sweet Rest Graveyard. Mr. and Mrs. Wolverton-Manning were standing in the shadows by Feris Wolfschmidt's tomb. The sun had just set behind the weeping willow trees.

"Why are we stopping here?" demanded Scarlett Angelina. "It's almost dark. I have to go home NOW!"

"Just wait here, you'll be home soon," Ralph said as he got out of the car. He put on a black mask, straightened his chauffeur's cap, and walked over to the tomb where Scarlett's parents were waiting. "Got the money?"

"It's all here in this bag," Mr. Wolverton-Manning said.

"Where is our daughter?" cried Mrs. Wolverton-Manning.

"She's in the car. You can have her back when I've counted my money," Ralph said. He pulled a wad of bills out of the sack and began counting. "She's a nice kid, but a little strange."

"It runs in the family," Scarlett's father replied. "Please, we must have her back now, it's getting dark." On the other side of the graveyard a full moon was rising.

"Hold on a minute, I'm counting," said Ralph.

Mr. Wolverton-Manning looked upset. "I'm afraid I can't do that much longer-er-r-r-R-R-RWO-O-O-O!" he howled, as his teeth grew sharper, his nails grew longer, and his face grew hairier. Mrs. Wolverton-Manning was smiling the famous Wolverton smile, complete with fangs, and her eyes were large and yellow.

Ralph screamed—"Eeeyyahh!"—and dropped the money bag. He ran back to the long black car with the two Wolverton-Mannings snapping at his heels.

"Hold on, kid, we're getting out of here!" he shouted as he zoomed the car toward the gates of the graveyard. "Werewolves! I can't believe those people are werewolves!"

And in the backseat Scarlett Angelina said, "GGGGRRRR."